"Nicodemus, the cat, is missing. We need to search for him," Alex explained.

"Hey, what do you say we check in there?" Mark pointed to a shed in Dan's yard.

Zack pulled open the shed door and the children whisked inside. Mark pulled the door closed. As soon as it shut, they heard a sudden rattle and a click outside the door. The children stared at each other in alarm.

Alex kicked the door. They twisted the doorknob in all directions. The door did not budge.

"It's locked!" they shouted. "We are trapped!"

Mint Cookie Miracles

NANCY S. LEVENE
Illustrated by Michelle Dorenkamp

Chariot Books
David C. Cook Publishing Co.

A Wise Owl Book
Published by Chariot Books,
an imprint of David C. Cook Publishing Co.
David C. Cook Publishing Co., Elgin, Illinois 60120
David D. Cook Publishing Co., Weston, Ontario

MINT COOKIE MIRACLES
© 1988 by Nancy S. Levene for text and Michelle
Dorenkamp for illustrations.

Designed by GraphCom Corporation
First printing, 1988
Printed in the United States of America
93   5

Library of Congress Cataloging-in-Publication Data
Levene, Nancy S., 1949—
    Mint cookie miracles.
    "A Wise owl book"—
    Summary: Alex's prayers are answered when she
manages to resolve a bad situation concerning an
elderly couple, their wonderful cat, and a neighborhood
bully.
    [1. Christian life—Fiction.   2. Bullies—Fiction]
I. Dorenkamp, Michelle, ill.   II. Title.
PZ7.L5724Mi 1988   [Fic]   88-11902
ISBN 1-55513-514-5

To my Lord, Jesus Christ,
who so faithfully keeps me on His path
and
To Lindsay Mayton,
whose sisterly love helps me to walk on it.

I love the Lord because He hears my prayers and answers them. Because he bends down and listens, I will pray as long as I breathe!

Psalm 116: 1, 2
The Living Bible

ACKNOWLEDGMENTS

Thank you Mom and Dad and Cara for all your interest and encouragement. Again, I thank Vicky and Karen for their word processing help. Thank you, Patti Kupka, for your wonderful friendship and for fanning the flames of enthusiasm.

CONTENTS

CHAPTER 1

Kidnapped

Alex watched as her father helped Mr. Mayton load suitcases and overnight bags into the trunk of his car. Mr. Mayton was taking his daughter, Sarah, and Alex's older sister, Barbara, to the Ozarks for a few days.

"She gets to swim in a lake and water ski and go to Silver Dollar City and everything," Alex grumbled to herself. "And I'm stuck here with nothing to do!"

Alex's best friend, Janie, had left on vacation last week and Alex missed her terribly. Things just didn't seem to go right when Janie was gone. And she would be gone for another whole week.

"Boy, am I glad to get out of here!" Alex

heard her older sister exclaim. "It has been incredibly boring. Nothing exciting ever happens around here."

Barbara and Sarah hopped into the back seat of the car. Barbara hung out the window. "Good-bye!" she called to Alex and her younger brother, Rudy.

Alex watched the car move down Juniper Street's hill and disappear around the curve. She kicked a rock into the street. "Brussels Sprouts! Barbara's right," she told Rudy. "Nothing exciting ever does happen around here."

"How about catching fireflies?" Rudy suggested.

"Oh, okay."

Alex followed her brother inside to get a jar. How could she expect Rudy to understand. After all, he was only six years old. *I guess he's too young to get bored,* thought Alex.

Alex and Rudy got busy collecting fireflies for the jar. Soon, however, Alex began to hear voices. The voices got louder and louder.

"HURRY UP!"

"RUN, KELLI, RUN!"

"QUICK! BEFORE THEY SEE US!"

All of a sudden, out of nowhere, running feet pounded over Alex's driveway and up the slope into her front yard. One, two, three, four, five children charged through the yard, knocking Rudy off his feet and spilling the jar from Alex's hand. All of the fireflies she had so patiently collected escaped from the jar.

"Brussels Sprouts!" hollered Alex. "What's the big idea?"

Nobody stopped to answer her. The crowd of children raced around a corner of Alex's house and disappeared.

Without hesitating, Alex charged around the corner after them. BAM! Like a bowling ball hitting the pins, Alex crashed into the children. Arms and legs flew as they bumped together and bounced apart. "OH! OUCH!" THUD!

Before anyone could stand up, Rudy bounded around the corner. He tripped, dove, and fell on top of the group.

"Why don't you watch where you're going?" someone yelled in Alex's ear.

Alex hopped to her feet, eyes blazing. She

found herself glaring into the eyes of a stranger.

"What do you mean, watch where I'm going?" she retorted. "This is my yard!"

Alex glanced quickly around. She recognized Zachary Logan and his younger brother, Mark. And there was Julie North and her little sister, Kelli. Zack and Julie had been in Alex's third grade class last year. Kelli had been in Rudy's first grade class. Zack, Mark, Julie, and Kelli lived down the hill, around the curve, and on the next street over from Alex.

Alex turned her attention back to the stranger. Who was he? He looked a little older than the rest of them.

Suddenly, Rudy howled, "FISHHEADS! My firefly got squished!" He held out his hand for Alex to see.

"Go catch another one, Goblin," Alex told Rudy.

"I'll go with you, Rudy," Kelli offered. She looked almost as upset as Rudy over the crushed bug.

"I think my little sister likes your little brother," Julie said, smiling at Alex shyly.

Alex smiled back at Julie. She hadn't seen Julie since the last day of school, over a month ago.

"Well," said Alex, not knowing quite what to say. "What are you guys doing here?"

"We are playing a game," answered Zack before Julie could reply.

"Yeah, it's great," added his brother, Mark. "We ring people's doorbells and run and hide before they open the door."

"You ought to see their faces when they

open the door and nobody's outside!" Zack broke in.

"Some of them come outside and look all around, but they can't see us because we're hiding," laughed Mark.

"And some of them slam the door shut right away and pull down the window shades," Zack chuckled.

Alex stared at the two boys. This "game" sounded like a good way to get into trouble.

"Why were you running through my yard?" Alex asked them.

"We just rang your next-door neighbor's doorbell," Mark explained.

Brussels sprouts! Her next door neighbors? That would be Jason's house. Jason was Rudy's best friend. Alex wondered what Jason's parents had thought when they opened the door and found nobody there.

"How come you're picking on my neighborhood?" Alex frowned. "What's the matter? Don't you have enough doorbells on your street?"

"We're expanding our territory," Zack told

14

her. "That's what Dan says. Right, Dan?" Zack nodded at the stranger. "This is Dan, Alex. He's from Chicago. He says everybody in Chicago rings doorbells and runs away."

"Everybody in Chicago?" Alex repeated in a low voice. That was hard to believe.

"Well, maybe not everybody," Dan admitted with a scowl. "But my friends and I did." He grinned slyly at Alex. "You want to join us?" he challenged.

"Yeah, come on, Alex!" cried Zack.

Alex hesitated.

"I think she's chicken," Dan sneered.

"Chicken?" Alex sputtered. How dare anyone call her "chicken!" Wasn't she the star pitcher for the Tornadoes? Hadn't she faced many threatening batters?

"BAWK! BAWK! Chicken!" teased Zack, hopping around Alex and flapping his arms.

Alex grabbed Zack by the neck and shook him. "Zack Logan! You know I am no chicken!"

"Okay, Alex, okay, take it easy," soothed Zack.

"Come on," Dan ordered. "I'm tired of hanging around here. It's time to attack Old Man Klunkett's doorbell."

"Oh, boy, Old Man Klunkett!" cried the other children. They scurried to the sidewalk.

"Coming, Alex?" called Julie.

Alex followed slowly. She decided she would see just what they were up to, and nobody was going to call her a chicken!

Rudy jogged ahead of Alex. His blonde hair sparkled under the street lights' reflection as he bobbed up and down beside Kelli. Rudy's real name was David, but he insisted on being called "Rudy." Alex usually called him "Goblin."

Why was everybody so excited to ring the Klunketts' doorbell, Alex wondered. Mr. and Mrs. Klunkett lived across Juniper Street and three houses down from Alex. They were old. They hardly ever came outside. Once in a while, Alex would see Mr. Klunkett stand on his front porch and call his cat. His cat was old, too. It would creep slowly and kind of stiff-legged to the door.

The other children had stopped and were

squatting behind a low hedge that ran on one side of the Klunketts' house. Alex caught up with them. Dan immediately yanked her down behind the hedge with the rest of them.

"What's the matter with you?" he hissed. "You want Old Man Klunkett to see you?" He began to whisper orders. "Okay, we circle around to the bushes on the other side of the driveway. After we ring the doorbells, we wait for Klunkett to pop out and start yelling. Then we run down the street fast! Got it?"

The children crawled to the end of the hedge and dashed, one by one, across the dark yard, dropping behind two large bushes on the other side of the driveway. Alex and Rudy followed.

When everyone was behind the bushes, Julie asked in a loud whisper, "Who gets to ring the doorbell?"

"How about you?" Dan whispered back.

"Me?" Julie looked pleased. "This will be my first time," she whispered excitedly to Alex.

Alex's stomach turned flip-flops as she watched Julie slowly creep up the walk to the Klunketts' door. Julie paused on the top step.

"Go on!" the boys commanded in hoarse whispers.

Rudy was so excited that he hopped up and down in front of the bushes. Alex reached out and pulled him down beside her.

Just as Julie's hand reached for the doorbell, something terrible happened. The Klunketts' front door suddenly burst open. Before Julie could run away, Mr. Klunkett grabbed her by the arm and pulled her inside his house.

"NOW I HAVE YOU!" Alex heard Mr. Klunkett roar. Julie screamed. The front door closed. There was sudden silence.

Alex, Dan, Zack, and Mark stared at each other in disbelief. Julie had been kidnapped!

"Let's get out of here!" Dan hissed. The older boys began running down Juniper Street's hill. Alex followed, holding onto Rudy's hand and half-dragging Kelli.

"Wait a minute! Hold up!" she called to the boys.

About halfway down the hill, the boys stopped running. Alex panted up to them. "You can't run away," she gasped. "You can't just leave Julie in there."

"Why not?" Dan snarled.

"Because she is your friend!" Alex snapped. "Friends don't leave each other in trouble."

"She's the one who got caught," Dan shrugged. "What do you want me to do about it—go up and knock on Mr. Klunkett's door and ask him to let Julie go?"

"Yeah," replied Alex.

"You gotta be crazy!" Dan turned to the other boys. "Let's go," he said.

"I don't believe this!" Alex cried. "Zack! Mark! We have to help Julie."

The two brothers looked down at their feet. Finally, Zack mumbled, "I'm sorry, Alex. I . . . uh, need to get home now."

With that, the three boys turned and raced down the street. Alex watched them until they disappeared around the curve at the bottom of the hill. She felt a sinking feeling as she slowly turned and climbed back up the hill toward the Klunkett house. Julie was a prisoner in that house. There was no one to help her but Alex. What should she do?

CHAPTER 2

Julie's Rescue

Alex stood in the middle of the street and stared at Mr. Klunkett's house. Why had Mr. Klunkett kidnapped Julie? Was she all right?

"Uh, Alex?" asked Rudy in a frightened whisper. "People don't murder kids for ringing their doorbells, do they?"

"Huh? No! That's ridiculous . . . at least I hope not," Alex whispered back.

"What are you going to do?" Rudy asked.

"I don't know, Goblin. Be quiet and let me think."

Kelli gripped Alex's hand tightly. Tears streamed down her face. "My poor sister," she moaned. "Please rescue my poor sister!"

Alex sighed. It looked like it was all up to her.

But what should she do?

"We aren't going in there, are we?" Rudy pointed at the Klunkett house. "I don't wanna get killed neither!"

"Goblin! Be quiet! Nobody's going to get killed."

Kelli began crying louder.

"Now see what you did?" Alex barked at her brother. "You are just making things worse."

Alex could feel the panic rise inside of her. Always before, whenever she was in trouble, she would ask Jesus to help her. Maybe she should do that now.

"Lord Jesus," she prayed, "please help me. I don't know what to do."

All at once, Alex had an idea. "Come on," she said to Rudy and Kelli. "We are going to get Dad."

Alex, Rudy, and Kelli banged into the front hallway of the Brackenbury home. To their right, a curved stairway led from the hallway to the bedrooms. The left side of the hallway opened into a large living room.

The children raced into the living room.

Mother sat on the sofa. She put down the newspaper she had been reading.

"Alex, Rudy, I was just getting ready to call you inside," Mother said. "It's almost nine o'clock. Why, who is this little girl?"

"Mom, this is Kelli. Something terrible has happened," groaned Alex.

"Yeah," burst out Rudy, "Julie's been kidnapped and maybe even killed!"

Kelli cried loud choking sobs.

Father, hearing the noise, hurried into the room. "What's going on, Firecracker?" he asked. "Firecracker" was Father's nickname for Alex.

"I was trying to explain until the Goblin opened his big mouth," Alex stomped her foot.

Mother sat Kelli beside her on the sofa and put her arm around her. "Alex, please tell us what has happened. Rudy, sit down and let Alex talk."

Alex told her parents about the children ringing the neighbors' doorbells and running away. She told them how Julie had been caught by Mr. Klunkett and how the boys had run away.

"And Julie's still in there," cried Alex. "You don't think Mr. Klunkett will hurt her, do you?"

"No, I'm sure he won't," Father answered. "I don't know Mr. Klunkett very well, but he seems like a nice man. However, I think we had better go over there right away." Father paused and looked closely at Rudy and Alex. "Before we go, I want to be sure that my children have not been ringing doorbells and running away."

"I never even heard of doing it until tonight," Alex told her father. "Rudy and I did go over to the Klunketts' with the other kids tonight and I'm sorry for that."

"Me too," Rudy added.

"Okay," Father smiled. "Let's go rescue Julie."

Rudy led the way down the street to the Klunketts' house. When they reached the front steps, Rudy quickly stepped behind his father. Kelli held Mother's hand.

Father rang the doorbell. Alex wished she could hide behind Father's legs like Rudy. But she did not want to look like a scaredy cat.

The front door opened. Mr. Klunkett peered out at them. He was a large man, taller and heavier than Father. Alex's knees shook.

"Hello," said Mr. Klunkett.

"Good evening," Father responded. He introduced himself and Mother and the children. Then he said, "I was told that you had some, uh, small visitors here tonight."

"Yes, I did have visitors, if that's what you want to call them," replied Mr. Klunkett rather gruffly. "Those children have been pestering my wife and me for several nights now. I caught one of them though—a little girl. Wish I would have caught one of those boys instead."

"Is the girl still in your house?" Father asked.

"No, no. I sent her on home," said Mr. Klunkett. "She seemed rather frightened. I don't think she will try ringing my doorbell again."

"Oh, dear," exclaimed Mother. "This is her younger sister, Kelli. I imagine her parents are quite worried about her. We had better call them."

"Well, come in and use my telephone," Mr. Klunkett invited. He held the door open wide.

Alex passed through the front door of the Klunkett home and caught her breath. A white-haired lady was sitting in a wheelchair in the living room. A brightly colored blanket covered her knees.

"Come in, come in," the lady called to them. "My, my, we are having lots of company tonight."

Mr. Klunkett introduced everyone to his wife and then showed Mother and Kelli where the telephone was.

Mrs. Klunkett reached for Alex and Rudy's hands and held them tightly. "What sweet-looking children," she exclaimed.

Alex and Rudy giggled nervously.

"I don't get to see children very often," Mrs. Klunkett told them. "Our grandchildren live so far away."

Alex stared down at that kindly old face and the wrinkled hand that held her own hand. She liked Mrs. Klunkett. The elderly lady's face shone with friendliness and her eyes sparkled.

Alex tried to count the "smile wrinkles" around Mrs. Klunkett's eyes. Once Father had said that she could tell the happy people from the sad people by counting their smile wrinkles. Mrs. Klunkett had lots of them. Alex wondered if Mrs. Klunkett ever felt sad about having to sit in a wheelchair. She felt especially ashamed of her friends for bothering this kind old lady.

Suddenly a little red ball bounced into Mrs. Klunkett's lap! Where had it come from? Alex looked up. Right above Mrs. Klunkett hung a bookcase. And on the top shelf of the bookcase stretched an orange and white cat. Its tail hung over the edge of the shelf. Its green eyes stared cooly down at Alex.

"Nicodemus!" laughed Mrs. Klunkett. "He's an old tease. He just loves to bat his toys off of his shelf and into my lap. That's why I sit here under his shelf."

"That's his shelf?" Rudy asked in wonder.

"Yes, we call it the Nicodemus Shelf," replied Mrs. Klunkett. "Every evening, Mr. Klunkett lines up all of the cat's toys across that shelf and, one by one, Nicodemus knocks them

off into my lap. It's a game we play."

"Really?" cried Alex. "That's amazing!"

"How does he get up there?" Rudy had to lean his head back and stand on tiptoe just to see the cat.

"Believe it or not, Nicodemus used to be able to jump from the floor all the way to the top shelf," Mrs. Klunkett chuckled. "Then one day he missed and crashed to the floor. He was very upset about that so Mr. Klunkett built him his own staircase. It goes all the way to the top shelf. Do you see it?"

Alex and Rudy peered behind Mrs. Klunkett. A table stood to the left of the bookshelves. On the table sat a set of small wooden steps that climbed to the first shelf. A second set of steps reached from the first shelf to the mantel above the fireplace. A third set led from the mantel to the top shelf.

"Brussels sprouts," gasped Alex. "A stairway to the ceiling."

"I'd like to go up those steps," wished her brother.

Just then Mother and Kelli returned to the living room. "Kelli's parents are coming to get her," Mother announced.

"Is Julie coming, too?" asked Alex.

"I think so."

Before long, a car pulled into the Klunketts' driveway. Mr. Klunkett opened the door for Julie and her parents.

"My! I haven't had so much excitement for a long time," Mrs. Klunkett exclaimed. She hurried to the kitchen for cookies and drinks. Alex followed her. Alex was fascinated by Mrs. Klunkett's electric wheelchair. All she had to do was push a button and away it went.

Soon, everyone sat in the living room and munched Mrs. Klunkett's mint cookies. They all agreed that they were the best cookies they had ever tasted.

"Well, thank you," Mrs. Klunkett replied to their compliments. "They are made from an old family recipe."

The conversation turned to Dan and his idea of ringing doorbells and running away.

"We had no idea it was going on," Julie's parents told Mr. and Mrs. Klunkett. "We are awfully sorry."

"That's all right," Mrs. Klunkett replied cheerfully. "It all turned out well. See, we have made several new friends tonight."

On the way home, Alex said to her parents, "You know, Mrs. Klunkett was right. Everything did turn out good. Isn't that funny? Tonight started out bad, but turned out good in the end."

"You had something to do with that, Firecracker," her father told Alex. "When Julie was in trouble, you came and got me. You didn't run away like the boys did. That was the right thing to do."

"Yeah," Alex agreed. "At first, I didn't know what to do, so I prayed to Jesus and He made me think of you. So I asked you to help us."

"Good for you, Firecracker," boomed Father. "I'm glad you asked the Lord to help you. He always helps us out of trouble."

Alex was silent for a moment. Then she said, "You know, those boys missed out on the good part of tonight by running away. They probably feel pretty rotten for running out on Julie—at least I bet Zack and Mark do. I don't think Dan feels bad about anything he does!"

"I wouldn't be too sure about that," Mother spoke up. "People who get their fun out of hurting other people are usually pretty miserable themselves."

"Really?" Alex was surprised. "Dan doesn't seem miserable. He just seems mean!"

"People don't just get mean, Alex," Mother replied. "Usually, something happens to make them mean. Dan might act mean to hide some

30

kind of hurt inside himself."

"Like what?" Alex wanted to know.

"I don't know, but God knows. Maybe you could say a prayer for Dan," Mother suggested.

That night at bedtime, Alex added at the end of her prayers, "Lord Jesus, please help Dan not to be so mean anymore."

CHAPTER 3

Bonzai
Pizza

The next day, when Alex came home from swim team practice, she found Julie and Kelli sitting on her doorstep. Alex was glad to see Julie. She needed someone to play with while Janie was gone.

"You wanna see my new cricket?" Rudy hollered out the car window to Kelli. "I just got him at the pool!"

Alex and Mother rolled their eyes at each other.

"Hi," Alex called to Julie.

"Hi," Julie answered, "Can you play?"

"Sure, just let me change clothes. Come on up to my room."

The two girls climbed the curvy staircase that led to the bedrooms. A few minutes later, Alex clattered back down the stairs.

"Mom," she hollered, running to the kitchen. "Julie and I want to make something for Mr. and Mrs. Klunkett. Will you take us to the shopping mall?"

"Wait a minute, hold on," her mother laughed. "Why do you need to go to a shopping mall?"

"To get a pattern, of course," Alex answered. "You know, a stuffed animal pattern. We want to make a cat for the Klunketts."

"Hmmmmm, I might be able to do that," Mother said slowly. "Of course, it means that we would have to take Rudy and Kelli along."

"Great!" cried Alex. She ran back to the stairway. "Julie, we can go! We can go! Thanks, Mom!" she called over her shoulder.

Alex, Julie, Rudy, and Kelli sat in the back seat of the Brackenbury station wagon. After Mother pulled into a parking space at the Kingswood Shopping Center, she turned to look at the children. "This is the rule," she told them. "We all stay together while we shop. No one is to go off on their own. It that understood?"

The children nodded their heads.

"Are you sure you understand, Rudy?" Mother asked him again.

"Aw, Mom," Rudy complained. "I only got lost once."

"Yeah, and it took us an hour and a half to find you," Alex reminded him.

Inside the shopping mall, Mother headed straight for the Crafts and Thread store. There, Alex and Julie picked out a cat pattern and some material. The material was blue and white checked.

"Whoever heard of a blue and white cat?" scoffed Rudy. "It won't look at all like Nico . . . Nico . . ."

"Nicodemus," Alex finished for him. "And blue happens to be my favorite color."

"You oughta get orange," Rudy insisted.

"There is no orange, Goblin. Now be quiet!" Alex hissed.

Mother paid for the material and the pattern and they left the store.

"Where are we going now?" Alex asked her mother.

"I'm hungry!" Rudy said in a loud voice. Mother looked at her watch. "It's only eleven o'clock. Let me look around for a little bit and then we will all have lunch."

The children followed Mother into a big department store. Mother walked swiftly through the purse and hat section and around a corner to the jewelry department.

The children were right behind her until Rudy stopped to try on a red hat with pink feathers. He looked so funny that each of the girls decided to try on a hat, too.

They didn't miss Mother at all until Rudy asked, "Where's Mom?"

"Brussels sprouts!" cried Alex, "You mean she got lost?"

"Mom!" Rudy called in a high, screeching voice. "HEY, MOM!"

"MOM!" Alex yelled in an even louder voice.

"Excuse me, may I help you?" a finger tapped Alex on the shoulder. Alex looked up.

A large, redheaded woman stared down at her. The woman was not smiling.

"May I help you?" the woman repeated.

Alex gulped. "We can't find our mother," she tried to explain.

"Come with me, please," ordered the woman. She started to walk away but soon stopped. The children did not follow her.

"Come with me, please," the woman said again.

"I'm sorry," Alex replied, "but my parents have told us never to go anywhere with a stranger."

Just then a familiar voice called, "Alex! Rudy!" Alex looked up to see Mother hurrying toward them.

"Oh! Thank goodness I have found you," Mother sighed when she reached them. "Where have you been?"

"We have been right here the whole time," Alex told her. "We only tried on a couple of hats. We didn't know where you went."

"Yeah," Rudy quickly added, "we didn't get lost, Mom. You did!"

A slow smile began to cover Mother's face. "I guess I did lose you, didn't I? I'm sorry." Mother thanked the store clerk and they quickly left the store.

They made their way to the other end of the shopping mall where Mother bought pizza for everybody.

"My piece is too big," complained Kelli. "I can't pick it up."

"Here, let me fix it!" Rudy cried. Before anyone could stop him, he gave Kelli's pizza a mighty karate chop. "BONZAI!" Tomato sauce, onions, and pepperoni splashed all over the table.

"Rudy!" Mother yelled.

"Oh, Goblin!" Alex covered her face.

People at other tables around them began to chuckle.

An embarrassed Mother marched Rudy to a restroom to wash his hands. Alex and Julie helped Kelli put her pizza back together. The girls broke into hysterical giggles.

"I don't think there's anyone as funny as Rudy," gasped Kelli.

"What a karate chop!" laughed Julie.

"Bonzai!" giggled Alex.

Mother soon led Rudy back to the table. He was red-faced and very quiet.

"Did you spank him?" Alex asked her mother.

"Never mind," Mother replied. They ate their pizzas in silence, except that now and then a giggle escaped from the girls.

When they had finished eating Mother said, "Well, Rudy, this has been a new experience. Never before have I seen anyone karate chop a pizza!"

They all laughed, even Rudy.

Back home, Mother helped Alex and Julie put the cat together. Julie cut the material while Alex stitched it together.

"Alex, don't lean so close to the sewing machine," warned Mother. "You might get your finger caught under the needle."

"Aw, Mom, I'll be careful," Alex replied. "Whoa!" she shouted. She had accidentally pushed the reverse button on the machine and the needle had run backwards off the material.

"Brussels sprouts," she groaned. "Mom, you gotta fix this."

"Hand it over," sighed Mother. She had "fixed" Alex's stitches several times before.

Alex tried to pass the material to Mother but couldn't. It seemed to be stuck to her T-shirt.

"Hey, what's going on?" she cried.

"Alex, I think you have sewn your T-shirt to the cat!" Mother laughed.

Alex jumped up out of her chair. The blue and white material hung from the bottom edge of her T-shirt.

Julie and Mother could hardly stop giggling. Mother helped Alex rip the material from her T-shirt and finish the rest of the machine stitching.

"Now, we get to stuff it," Alex told Julie. "That's the best part."

"I think I'll let you girls do the best part yourselves," smiled Mother. She left the room.

Alex and Julie began to stuff the cat. Little bits of snow-white stuffing flew everywhere as the girls pushed them into the tiny points of the cat's ears, into its head, body, and finally, the long tail.

Alex's puppy, T-Bone, was delighted with the stuffing project. He raced from one end of the room to the other, chasing the little white bits as they floated through the air.

"Look at your dog," Julie laughed. "He looks more like a white dog than a black dog now."

"Brussels sprouts, T-Bone, you're a mess!" cried Alex. Pieces of stuffing clung to the dog's normally black fur.

"He is polka-dotted," Julie giggled.

"Woof! Woof!" T-Bone barked and ran over to the girls. He grabbed the stuffed cat's tail in his mouth.

"T-Bone! Cut that out!" Alex hollered. "Give me that tail."

The more Alex pulled on the tail, the harder T-Bone held onto it.

"Oh great, he thinks I'm playing tug of war with him," Alex told Julie. She gave an extra hard pull. The tail pulled free from T-Bone's mouth, but Alex fell backwards and knocked the giant bag of stuffing off the sofa. The bag tipped upside down and landed on T-Bone's head!

"Oh, no!" the girls hollered. Now the only part of the puppy that was not white were his eyes.

"What in the world is going on in here?" exclaimed Mother as she came to the door. "Oh, my goodness!" she gasped.

T-Bone wagged his tail and galloped over to Mother.

"T-Bone!" Mother cried. "Is that really you? You look like a . . . like a . . ."

41

"Like a sheep!" Alex finished for her. They all laughed.

"Looks like we have some cleaning to do, girls," Mother told them.

"I think we better clean the dog first," Julie giggled.

"I think you are right," Mother agreed.

It took them until late afternoon to clean the dog and the room—and to finish stuffing the cat.

"It's finished!" Alex and Julie exclaimed in relief.

"It's too fat!" Rudy scowled as he entered the room.

"Be quiet!" Mother, Julie, and Alex told him.

Alex and Julie proudly carried the stuffed cat down the street to the Klunketts'. Rudy and Kelli tagged along behind.

"Look! There's Zack and Mark!" Alex shouted. She waved to the two boys as they wheeled their bicycles up the Juniper Street hill.

The boys waved back. They had almost reached one another when suddenly a big, brown dog charged in front of Zack's bike and knocked him to the ground.

The dog sped over the front hedge of the Klunketts' yard and ran straight for Nicodemus, who was sunning himself on the front walk.

Nicodemus yowled, hissed, and spit, but the old cat was no match for the dog. The dog chased Nicodemus to the hedge and back again, all the while snapping at the cat's tail.

The children screamed. It seemed that at any moment the dog would catch Nicodemus and would swallow him up in its big jaws!

CHAPTER 4

Mean Machine

The children screamed and screamed again. The dog was closing in fast on Nicodemus. The old cat wouldn't last much longer.

Mr. Klunkett ran out of the house carrying a broom. Zack leaped over the hedge and cracked a large stick across the dog's back. At the same time, Alex threw a stone and hit the dog on its nose.

The dog yelped and stopped running. For a moment, it looked like it might attack Zack, but Mr. Klunkett gave an extra loud holler and swung his broom. The dog raced out of the yard and down the street.

"Thank you! Thank you so much for saving Nicodemus," gasped Mr. Klunkett. He shook hands with Zack and Alex.

"Where is Nicodemus?" Alex asked, turning around and looking for the cat.

"Up there!" Rudy shouted.

They all looked skyward. An orange and white ball of fur clung to the topmost branches of a tall elm tree.

Mr. Klunkett laughed. "Nicodemus hasn't climbed that tree in years."

"I'll get him," offered Zack.

"You may have to," Mr. Klunkett replied. "After such a scare, Nicodemus may not come down for a week!"

Zack quickly climbed the tree and plucked Nicodemus off of the branch. He climbed back down and handed the frightened cat to Mr. Klunkett.

"Won't you come inside?" he asked the children. "Mrs. Klunkett will want to thank Nicodemus's rescuers."

The children followed him into the house. Mrs. Klunkett sat in her wheelchair in front of the window.

"Oh, thank you!" she exclaimed when she

saw them. "What brave children. I saw it all from the window."

Mrs. Klunkett's eyes glistened with happiness. Alex decided that she would gladly tangle with a hundred mean dogs to make this old lady happy.

"We brought you a present, Mrs. Klunkett," Alex said shyly.

"A present?" Mrs. Klunkett looked surprised.

Alex motioned to Julie, and Julie handed Mrs. Klunkett the stuffed cat that they had made.

"We made it ourselves," Alex said proudly.

"Why, it's beautiful," exclaimed Mrs. Klunkett. "I will treasure it always. Thank you."

"A blue cat." Rudy rolled his eyes. "I told them to make it orange."

Mrs. Klunkett laughed. She wheeled herself into the kitchen and came back with a platter of her freshly baked mint cookies.

"Ummmmm, do you make these cookies every day?" Rudy asked delighted.

"Just about," Mrs. Klunkett laughed. "It's my specialty."

"What's that?" Rudy pointed to an object sitting on the dining room table.

"That, my boy, is a train engine—a Union Pacific, to be exact," answered Mr. Klunkett.

The children crowded around the table to inspect the small, shiny black engine.

"Do you have any cars to hook onto it?" Rudy asked Mr. Klunkett.

Mr. Klunkett winked at Mrs. Klunkett. "Follow me," he told the children.

They marched through a family room and down some steps to the basement. Alex opened her eyes wide as Mrs. Klunkett slowly steered her wheelchair down a ramp that was built to the side of the basement stairway.

When they reached the basement, the children gasped in delight. On giant tables wound many miles of train tracks. They crisscrossed and curved through miniature cities, country villages, and farmland. They looped through hills and over mountains, rivers, and ponds. Highways and dirt roads

47

intersected the train tracks. At each intersection was a railway crossing. Houses, stores, factories, and gas stations lined the city streets.

"Even a little church," Alex breathed in wonder.

"We have several churches," Mrs. Klunkett pointed out. "Every village needs a church."

"Wow, look at the greenhouse!" Mark exclaimed. He pointed to a little, glass greenhouse. A tiny man held a bush in his arms. Rows of trees, bushes, and flowers surrounded the greenhouse.

"There are ducks swimming in this pond," shouted Zack, "and a fisherman."

"Yeah, but look at this mountain tunnel!" cried Rudy.

Suddenly, Mr. Klunkett clapped an engineer's hat on his head and boomed, "ALL ABOARD!" He flipped several switches and the trains began to move.

Alex counted one, two, three, four, five trains and two trolleys. They quickly picked up speed. The trains whizzed through the countryside, climbed the mountains, and shot through the tunnels. With loud whistles, they roared under and over each other, sometimes barely missing one another. The trolleys clanged up and down the city streets, ringing their bells.

"Now watch this," Mr. Klunkett shouted over the noise. He turned off the overhead lights. Darkness filled the corners of the basement.

"Oooooooooh!" the children cried in delight. Lights twinkled in every house. Stained glass windows sparkled in the churches. Street lights shone. The railway crossings and traffic lights blinked red or green. The trolley cars lit up, showing outlines of people sitting inside. Engines beamed flashes of light at one another as they continued their race around the tracks.

All too soon, Mr. Klunkett turned the lights back on and stopped the trains.

"Can we come back and see them again?" Rudy asked him.

"Of course you can," Mr. Klunkett answered.

The children thanked him and Mrs. Klunkett

for showing them the trains. "And for the mint cookies," Kelli added.

Mr. and Mrs. Klunkett thanked the children for helping to rescue Nicodemus from the dog. As they left the Klunkett house, Mark, Zack, Alex, Julie, Kelli, and Rudy waved good-bye to Mr. and Mrs. Klunkett. They were all friends now. Alex was glad.

"Well, isn't that sweet—waving good-bye to Old Man Klunkett?" snarled a voice behind them.

The children whirled around. Dan was leaning against a car that was parked across the street. His eyes were narrowed into tiny slits. Alex thought she had never seen such mean-looking eyes before.

"Been visiting Old Man Klunkett?" Dan hissed at Zack.

Zack squirmed uncomfortably. "He's not such a bad guy," he finally replied.

"You oughta see his trains," Mark spoke up. "They are really . . ."

"SHUT UP!" Dan hollered. "Old Man Klunkett's a loser!"

"How would you know?" Alex replied hotly. "You don't even know him."

Dan took a step toward Alex. " 'Cuz he's a grown-up! Get it? All grown-ups are losers!" He gave Alex a shove.

"My dad's a grown-up and he's not a loser!" Rudy shouted at Dan.

"Shut up, short stuff." Dan pushed Rudy to the ground.

"Leave my brother alone!" Alex yelled at Dan.

"Who's going to make me?" Dan retorted.

"We are!" Zack and Mark shouted. They moved to stand beside Alex.

"Yeah, we are!" echoed Julie and Kelli.

Dan glared at them all, then backed away. "Aw, you're all a bunch of losers," he growled. He turned and walked away.

The others watched him stalk down the hill.

"Boy, what a creep!" Julie exploded.

"Yeah!" Mark agreed. "Dan's a mean machine!"

Alex was silent for a moment. "I don't know," she said slowly. "My mom says Dan might be acting mean to hide a hurt inside of himself."

"Does she mean like a busted stomach or something?" Rudy wanted to know.

Alex laughed. "No, Goblin, not that kind of hurt. I think she means more like . . . uh . . . hurt feelings."

"Hurt feelings?" Julie questioned.

"Yeah, you know . . . like something horrible happened to Dan to make him so mean."

"Really?" Zack thought a moment. "I know he doesn't have a dad. And his mom works all day and sometimes at night, too. Dan just kind of hangs around by himself.''

"Maybe he's lonely," Julie suggested.

"Lonely? Could being lonely make you mean?" Alex wondered.

Just then, Mother called, "Alex! Rudy! Time for dinner!"

"See you later," Alex told the others. She and Rudy hurried home.

At dinner, Alex and Rudy told their parents about Nicodemus and the dog, and about meeting Dan outside the Klunketts' house.

"Can being lonely make somebody mean?" Alex asked her parents.

"Well, it might," Mother answered thoughtfully. "Do you think that is Dan's problem?"

"Maybe," Alex replied. "Zack says he is by himself a lot because his mother works. And," she added, "he doesn't have a father."

"Oh, that's too bad," Mother said. "Children need a father figure."

"What's a father figure?" Rudy and Alex asked together.

Before Mother could answer, Father jumped

out of his chair. "A father figure is a father with a great figure—like me!" He held his arms up to show them his muscles.

"Oh, Dad!" giggled Alex and Rudy.

"Oh, brother," Mother sighed.

"A father figure is an important man in a child's life. He is the child's model. The child learns how to act and behave by watching his father figure," explained Father.

"Are there mother figures, too?" Alex asked.

"Yes, we need them, too."

"You and Mom are our mother and father figures," said Alex, "But what if you don't have a mother or a father?"

"Then a child can learn from another grown-up—like an aunt or an uncle, or a grandma or a grandpa, or even a neighbor," Father answered.

Alex thought about that for a moment. "That must be it! Dan needs a father figure to show him how to act. He sure isn't doing so good on his own!"

Father laughed. "Well, you know, Firecracker, Dan really does have a Father—the same Father that we all have."

"You mean God, don't you?" asked Alex.

"Yes, He is the greatest Father anyone can ever have. By reading the Bible, we can learn how our Father in heaven wants us to act."

"Why don't we say a prayer for Dan right now?" suggested Mother.

The family joined hands and bowed their heads as Father prayed, "Dear Heavenly Father, we ask You to help Dan. Please bring him a special person—someone to be his father figure. Thank you for hearing our prayer. We pray in the name of Jesus. Amen."

Almost immediately, the telephone rang.

"Hello," Mother answered it.

Father, Alex, and Rudy stared at Mother as her face became more and more upset.

"Yes, Mr. Klunkett, we will come right over. I am terribly sorry about this. Good-bye." Mother hung up the telephone.

"That was Mr. Klunkett," Mother told them. "He thinks that someone has stolen Nicodemus."

CHAPTER 5

A Cat Robber

"Someone has stolen Nicodemus?" Alex and Rudy cried.

"What?" exclaimed Father. "Who in the world would steal a cat from such nice old people?"

Alex and Rudy looked at each other. "Dan!" they both answered.

"Oh, surely not," Mother said. "He can't be that mean."

"Oh, yes, he can," they assured her.

"Well," Mother shrugged, "maybe you are right. Come on, I told Mr. Klunkett we would come right over. Poor man, he is so upset."

When they reached the Klunketts' house, they found Mr. Klunkett in his front yard. He told them what had happened. "I let Nicodemus outside early this evening. Crazy cat! I didn't think he would go outside so soon after tangling with that dog.

"I meant to stay outside with him," Mr. Klunkett continued, "but the telephone rang. I ran inside to answer the telephone. When I came back outside, Nicodemus was gone!

"I called and called his name. He always comes when I call his name. Then I heard footsteps running down the street. A boy was running as fast as he could go down the hill. He was carrying a big sack of some kind. Somehow I know Nicodemus was in that sack."

"Did you recognize the boy?" Father asked.

"Never got a good look at him," replied Mr. Klunkett. "He was too far away."

"Was he bigger than me?" Alex asked Mr. Klunkett.

"Well, yes, I would say so," Mr. Klunkett rubbed his chin.

"Did he have black hair?" asked Rudy excitedly.

"He had dark hair," Mr. Klunkett admitted.

"Dan!" the children cried.

"Now, Alex and Rudy, we do not know for sure that Dan took Nicodemus. We cannot accuse him without proof," warned Father.

"But, Dad, who else would do it?" argued Alex.

"I am sure I don't know. I can't imagine anyone stealing someone else's cat." Father looked disgusted.

"Well, all I know is that Nicodemus is gone and things won't be the same around here without him," sighed Mr. Klunkett. "My poor wife is just miserable."

Poor Mrs. Klunkett, Alex thought sadly. *She loves Nicodemus so much.*

"Dad!" Alex stomped her foot. "Aren't we going to do anything about this?"

Her father smiled down at her. "Yes, we are, Firecracker. I think it is time we paid Dan a visit."

They said good-bye to Mr. Klunkett and went home to get the car. Father drove the car down Juniper Street, around the curve, and onto Maple Street.

"Which house is Dan's?" he asked Alex.

"I have never been there," Alex replied, "but Julie said he lives in between her house and Zack's house. It must be that white one."

Father pulled into the driveway of the white house. Mother, Alex, and Rudy followed him to the front door. Father rang the doorbell.

A pretty, but tired-looking, woman answered the door. She looked surprised to see so many people on her doorstep.

Father introduced himself and his family. He then asked if Dan lived there.

"Why, yes," Dan's mother said, looking puzzled.

"May I speak with him?" Father asked politely. Dan's mother invited them inside. She called Dan's name loudly.

Alex heard an upstairs door slam and a clatter of feet on the stairway. Dan scowled when he saw Alex and Rudy. But when he saw Father, the scowl changed to a look of surprise and then fear.

"Dan," Father said in a low but stern voice, "we are looking for Mr. Klunkett's cat. Have you seen him?"

Dan looked away from Father. "No," he mumbled.

"Earlier this evening, a boy was seen running down the street, away from the Klunketts' house. He was carrying a large sack. The boy looked somewhat like you," Father told Dan.

Dan shrugged and said nothing. He gazed at the floor in front of him.

Father squatted down in front of Dan and looked up into his eyes. "Son," he said gently, "Mr. and Mrs. Klunkett are two old people who wouldn't hurt anyone. They have no children living with them. All they have is their cat. I will ask you one more time. Do you know where the cat is?"

Dan's face changed. For a moment it looked like he might say something further to Father, but the moment passed. His face grew hard again.

"NO!" Dan shouted. He turned and ran back up the stairs.

"Daniel!" his mother called after him.

"That's okay," sighed Father, "let him go."

"What is this all about?" asked Dan's

mother. "Who are the Klunketts?"

Father and Mother told her about Mr. and Mrs. Klunkett and how the children had rung their doorbell and run away.

"Oh, dear!" exclaimed Dan's mother. "I had hoped all that would stop. You see, we just moved here from Chicago and I thought a new neighborhood and new friends might help Dan to stay out of trouble."

"Maybe it will," encouraged Mother. "Give him some time. He might turn around."

"I don't know. It doesn't seem to be getting any better," Dan's mother sighed.

"Well, we can't always tell what will happen in the future," Father told her. "Maybe something good will come out of all this."

Back in the car, Alex fumed, "I know Dan took Nicodemus. I just know it!"

"Yeah," Rudy scowled and folded his arms across his chest. "Dan is a cat robber!" he exclaimed.

I think I agree with you," Father replied. "But until Dan admits it, there is nothing we can do."

"Well, I think he has hidden Nicodemus somewhere, and I am going to search the whole neighborhood tomorrow," Alex declared.

"Me, too!" exclaimed Rudy.

"All right," agreed Mother, "but just stay out of Dan's way for a while. He does not seem like someone you would want to tangle with."

The next morning, after swim team practice, Alex and Rudy rode their bicycles to Julie and Kelli's house. Dan was sitting on his front porch, tossing a ball in the air. Alex didn't look in his direction, but she could feel his stare as they parked their bikes and walked to Julie's front door.

"Brussels sprouts! You won't believe what has happened!" she exclaimed as soon as Julie opened the door.

Quickly, Alex and Rudy told Julie and Kelli about Nicodemus and about visiting Dan's house the night before. They repeated the story to Zack and Mark as soon as the boys came over.

"That's awful," exclaimed Mark. "Stealing a cat! What a creepy thing to do."

"Do you really think Dan stole Nicodemus?" Zack asked Alex.

"Yes," Alex answered. "You should have seen his face when my dad talked to him. He sure looked guilty."

"There must be something we can do," Julie wailed.

"We need to look for Nicodemus," Alex replied. "I am planning to search the whole neighborhood."

"We'll help you!" the others cried.

"Okay. We gotta search all the yards and bushes and knock on everybody's door and ask people if they've seen Nicodemus," Alex told them.

"But Alex," Rudy interrupted, "if Nicodemus was somewhere outside, wouldn't he just go home by himself?"

"Naw, Goblin. Dan probably put him in a cage or tied him up or something."

"We oughta search Dan's yard first," Zack suggested.

"Yeah, I know," Alex agreed. "But how are we going to do it without Dan seeing us?"

"We will just have to be sneaky," replied Zack. "Come on!"

The children rushed outside and peered through the trees into Dan's backyard. Everything seemed peaceful and quiet. The only sounds were birds chirping and insects buzzing. Dan was nowhere in sight.

"Hurry up," Alex motioned to the others. "We gotta do it before Dan sees us."

They ran as quietly as they could, ducking behind bushes and trees to keep out of sight.

"Look underneath all the bushes," Zack whispered loudly.

"Hey, what do you say we check in there?" Mark pointed to a shed that stood in a far corner of Dan's yard.

"Yeah," his brother breathed, "that's a perfect hiding place."

The children ran over to the shed. A padlock was attached to the door but it hung open.

"Do you think we ought to go in there?" Julie asked doubtfully. "My mom says it's wrong to go into other people's houses without being invited."

"I know, my mom says that, too," said Alex. "But I think we better. Nicodemus might be in there. Besides, this isn't a house—it's just an old shed."

Zack pulled open the shed door and the children whisked inside.

"Close the door," Mark ordered. "If Dan sees the door open, he will know somebody's in here."

"We better leave it open a little or it will be too dark in here," his brother said.

"But there's a window," Mark argued.

Zack shrugged. Mark pulled the door closed. As soon as it shut, they heard a sudden rattle and a click outside the door. The children stared at each other in alarm. That rattle and click had sounded like someone locking the padlock on the outside of the door.

Zack hurled himself at the door. Alex kicked at the door. Julie twisted the doorknob in all directions. The door did not budge.

"It's locked!" the children shouted. "The door's locked! We are trapped!"

CHAPTER 6

Trapped

A nasty howl of laughter sounded outside the door of the shed. "Ha, ha, ha! I got you now!"

"It's Dan!" yelled Mark. "He locked us in here!"

"Dan! You open this door right now!" Alex hollered.

More laughter rang out.

"Open this door!" Alex shouted again.

"I forgot the combination to the lock," Dan said.

"Dan, this is not funny! If you don't let us out, I am going to tell my mother and she will tell your mother," Julie cried.

"My mother is at work, Miss Know-it-all, and how are you going to tell your mother if you can't get outside?" Dan hissed through the crack in the door.

"Well, my dad will beat you up!" roared Rudy.

"Ha, ha, ha! I'm not afraid of your dumb dad," called Dan.

Rudy ran at the door in a rage. He hit the end of a rake that was hanging beside it. The rake crashed to the ground, barely missing his head.

Alex grabbed Rudy and pulled him away from the door. "Take it easy, Goblin. It's not going to do any good to get so mad."

"What if he never lets us out?" Kelli whimpered. "What if we're stuck in here forever?"

Julie put her arm around her little sister. "Don't worry," she told her, "we'll get out of here somehow."

"How about the window?" Mark suggested. "We could climb out that way."

"The window doesn't open," Zack answered.

"We could break it," his brother replied.

"Yeah . . ." Zack considered, "but it would be hard. For one thing, we can't even reach it."

"We could climb up on something," Mark looked around. "We could use that ladder over there."

"We could," Zack agreed, "but it would be dangerous. Glass would fly all over the place if we smashed the window."

"I'd rather not break the window," said Alex, "at least not until we run out of other ideas."

"Okay," Mark shrugged. "You got any other ideas?"

"We could all scream at the same time and see if anybody hears us," Alex suggested.

"It's worth a try," Julie said. "Maybe my mom will hear us."

They all took big breaths. Alex counted to three and everyone screamed as loud as possible.

"HELP! HELP! LET US OUT OF HERE!"

"Hey! Shut up in there!" Dan hollered through the door, but the children kept right on shouting.

Finally, one by one, they slumped to the

floor, gasping for breath. Their throats ached. Tiny drops of sweat rolled off their faces.

"Hey, Dan," Zack called through the crack in the door, "it's really hot in here."

"Aw, isn't that too bad," Dan growled back.

"Dan! We need to get some fresh air," Zack insisted.

"Yeah, and I'm thirsty," Rudy complained.

"Tough luck!" Dan yelled. "It's your own fault for sneaking into my shed!"

"It's your fault for locking us in here," screamed Alex. "We were only looking for the Klunketts' cat!" She raced to the door and kicked it angrily.

"Ow!" she grabbed her foot and fell to the floor. She could hear Dan laughing at her from outside the door.

After a while, the children grew quiet. They were hot and tired and couldn't think of anything more to do. Minutes crept by. They seemed like hours. The shed grew warmer and warmer as the sun burned down upon it. The air was heavy and hard to breathe.

Alex began to fear that they might suffocate inside the shed. She had heard how dangerous it was to be locked inside a trunk or an old refrigerator. Was being locked inside a shed just as bad?

"What should I do?" Alex asked herself over and over again. Then, like a bright light cutting through darkness, an answer flashed in her mind. It was one word—*pray!*

"Of course," Alex told herself. The Lord always helped her when she was afraid. She could count on Him.

"Dear Lord Jesus," Alex prayed silently, "please help us get out of this shed. Amen."

"Alex! What's the matter?" Rudy's voice shattered the silence.

Alex jumped. "What do you mean, Goblin?" she asked.

"You were sort of leaning over and you had your eyes closed," frowned Rudy.

"Oh, I was saying a prayer, Goblin. I was asking Jesus to help us get out of here."

"That's funny!" Zack interrupted. "I was doing the same thing."

Alex looked at him in surprise. "Are you a Christian?" she asked.

"You bet," he replied.

"Do you really think saying a prayer will help?" Julie wanted to know.

"It always works for me," Alex declared.

"Me, too," Zack agreed.

"You ought to try it," Alex told Julie. "Jesus said that if two or more people pray together and ask Him for the same thing, He will answer their prayers."

"Okay, I'll do it!" Julie bowed her head.

"Me, too," cried Mark, Kelli, and Rudy.

When she had finished praying, Julie asked, "Now what do we do?"

"We wait for God's answer," Zack told her simply.

The children grew quiet again. They leaned back against the shed walls.

"Hey, why aren't you making any noise in there?" Dan called through the crack in the door. Nobody bothered to answer him.

"Hey!" Dan hollered again. From where Alex was sitting, she could see Dan's shadow as

he paced back and forth in front of the door.

"Anybody still alive in there?" Dan shouted, sounding worried. Alex held a finger to her lips, motioning to the others to keep quiet.

Once or twice Dan fingered the padlock, as if he was deciding whether or not to unlock it. Suddenly, Alex heard the combination lock begin to spin.

At the same time, a woman's voice called from the yard next door. "Dan! Have you seen Julie and Kelli?"

"Mom!" Julie cried.

73

"Mom!" Kelli screamed.

Instantly, all of the children in the shed began shouting as loud as they could.

"Julie? Kelli?" Their mother's face peeked in through the crack of the shed door. "What in the world are you doing in there?"

"Dan locked us in here!" Julie called to her mother.

"He did?" Julie's mother exclaimed. "I wondered why he ran away so fast when I called his name!"

"Let us out of here, Mom," Kelli wailed. "I want out?"

"It's all right, Kelli," her mother soothed. "I'll get you out of there somehow. Who else is in there?"

"It's us!" cried Alex, Rudy, Zack, and Mark.

"Good heavens!" Julie's mother exclaimed. "How did Dan manage to lock all of you inside the shed?"

"We were looking for Nicodemus," replied Julie. She quickly explained all that had happened.

Julie's mother fiddled with the lock and tried spinning it every which way. Finally, she told the children, "I can't unlock it. I'll have to get some help."

"Wait, Mom," Julie cried. "Before you go, can you bring us some water? We're really thirsty."

"Water?" her mother repeated. "Wait a minute! I know just the thing!"

All of a sudden, the bottom of the shed door jerked outward and a long green object snaked its way in under the door.

"A hose!" Alex cried joyfully.

"Oh, turn it on! Quick!" they all shouted to Julie's mother.

A stream of water shot out of the end of the hose. Everyone rushed forward. Zack was the fastest. He grabbed the end of the hose and held his hand up. "Youngest goes first," he ordered. He passed it to Kelli and then to Rudy.

At last Alex had a chance to gulp down several big mouthfuls of water. She held her head under the hose. The cold water felt wonderful!

"I think I had better turn the hose off now," Julie's mother called before long. "I don't want to flood the shed."

"Why not?" grumbled Rudy. "It's only mean old Dan's shed."

"Yeah, but his mom would have to clean it up, and she's a nice lady," Zack told him.

"And besides, Goblin, we don't want to do anything mean just because somebody else does something mean to us," Alex reminded him.

"That's right. If you start doing mean things, you might end up just like Dan," warned Mark.

Rudy wrinkled his nose. He did not want to be like Dan. No way!

Julie's mother turned off the water. "I'm going to go call your mothers and I will try to find Dan. He's the only one who can unlock the padlock," she called to the children.

"What if you can't find him?" Kelli worried.

"Then we'll get you out another way," her mother assured her.

"My dad could bust down this door," Rudy suggested.

Julie's mother laughed. "I think we will try some other way first. Don't worry, I'll be right back." Then she added. "Don't go away!"

"Very funny, Mom," Julie retorted.

The children sat down to wait. They had to sit on boxes and overturned flower pots as the floor was now wet.

"Well, it worked," Julie said to Alex.

"What do you mean? What worked?" Alex asked.

"The prayers!" Julie answered. "As soon as we said the prayers, my mom came over!"

"Oh, yeah, sure. I knew it would work," Alex responded confidently.

"Really? You mean you really knew that God would get us out of here?" Julie looked surprised.

"Of course. God always answers prayer," Alex insisted.

"You mean God always gives you whatever you ask Him for?" Julie asked amazed.

"No, because sometimes I ask Him for the wrong thing," Alex answered.

"I don't understand," Julie frowned.

"Well, like, one time I told a whole bunch of lies. Then, I tried to get out of them and I asked God to help me. See, I just wanted Him to make all the lies disappear so that everything would be okay again," explained Alex.

"And did He make the lies disappear?" Julie asked.

"Well, sort of," Alex admitted. "But His real answer to my prayers was for me to tell the truth. Then, after I told the truth, the lies disappeared."

"Oh, so God wanted you to do it the right way," exclaimed Julie. "First, you had to tell the truth. Then, the lies disappeared."

"Right," Alex agreed.

All of a sudden, from outside the shed door, familiar voices were calling, "Alex! Rudy! Zack! Mark!"

"It's Mom!" Alex cried and leaped to her feet.

"Mom! Mom! Mom!" Rudy hollered through the crack in the door.

"Hey, Mom!" Zack and Mark yelled to their mother.

"I can't believe this," Alex heard her mother say.

"Where is Dan?" Zack's mother responded angrily. "I'd like a few words with that boy!"

"He has either run off or he is hiding in his house and won't answer the door," Julie's mother replied.

"Well, I don't think we can get this padlock off without Dan," sighed Alex's mother. "Children!" she called, "We are going to have to call the police."

CHAPTER 7

Dan
Disappears

Alex stared wide-eyed through the crack in the shed door as a large man dressed in a grey-blue uniform strode across the yard toward the shed.

"Brussels sprouts! He's got a gun and everything!" she whispered to the others.

"Let me see! Let me see!" hollered Rudy.

Everyone crowded around the door and peered outside.

The police officer introduced himself as Officer Rayburn. The mothers tried to explain to him what had happened.

"Stand back! Get away from the door!" Officer Rayburn called to the children. He held what looked like a small saw in his hand.

The children moved away from the door.

Soon, they could hear the saw rasp back and forth, back and forth.

"He's cutting the door down!" Rudy cried excitedly.

"No, I think he is cutting the lock," Zack told him.

With a last rasp, a rattle, and a clunk, the door swung open. Sunlight flooded the shed. The children were free.

"Hurray!" everyone cried. The children tumbled outside to hug their mothers. Alex looked at the outside of the shed door. Zack had been right. A big slice was cut through the padlock.

Officer Rayburn asked the children many questions about Dan. He wrote some things down in a notepad. He rang Dan's doorbell, but there was no answer.

"I will come back this evening and talk to his mother," Officer Rayburn told them.

Alex liked Officer Rayburn. She waved good-bye as he drove away in his police car.

"Someday, I'm going to be a policeman just like him," Rudy told her.

That night at dinner, Alex and Rudy described their adventure to Father.

"It was really kind of spooky," Alex admitted, "being stuck in that shed and not knowing if we would get out."

"But, Dad, I kept telling everybody that you could break down the door easy!" cried Rudy. "You could, couldn't you?"

"Easy," Father laughed, "with one hand tied behind my back!"

"Oh, brother," Mother sighed.

"Well, I'm glad you didn't have to break

down the door," Alex commented. "I mean, a broken padlock is better than a broken door, and Dan's mother has enough trouble with Dan without having to put a new door on her shed."

"I agree, Alex," said Mother. "I feel sorry for Dan's mother, and I feel sorry for Dan," she added.

"Sorry for Dan!" Rudy exploded. "I don't feel sorry for Dan! I feel like . . . like . . . giving him a good kick!"

They all laughed.

"I think your mother feels sorry for Dan because Dan must be awfully unhappy to be so mean and angry all the time," Father explained to Rudy.

"Yeah, well, he was gonna leave us in that shed forever until we died!" Rudy scowled.

"I don't think so," Alex said thoughtfully. "I really think Dan was going to open the lock for us." She smiled at the surprised looks on their faces. "Right before Julie's mom found us, we got real quiet and Dan seemed worried about us. He kept asking us if we were all right, and then, when nobody answered, it sounded like he started to open the lock."

"Really?" interrupted Mother.

"But Julie's mother called to him and he ran away," finished Alex.

"Hmmmmm," Mother said, "Dan may have a good side after all."

"Maybe," Alex replied. "Anyway, it happened right after we all said a prayer. I was sort of wondering if God had wanted Dan to open the lock and let us out, instead of Julie's mom finding us and calling the police and everything."

"That could be," Mother said.

"But can people spoil God's plans?" Alex asked her mother. "I mean, if God wanted Dan to open the lock but, instead, Julie's mother scared him away, then God's plan was spoiled, right?"

Her mother agreed.

"But that's not right!" Alex exclaimed. "Why would God let people spoil His plans? He's a lot bigger than they are!"

Her parents laughed.

"I agree with you, Firecracker," her father

chuckled. "It doesn't seem right that people should be able to spoil God's plans, but sometimes they do. You see, God gives us a choice. We can follow Him or not follow Him. When we follow Him, we fit into His plans and they don't get messed up. But when we don't follow Him, things can get in an awful mess."

"How do you know how to follow Him?" Rudy wanted to know.

"By reading the Bible and by praying," Father replied. "If we ask God to show us the way He wants us to go, then He will."

"But what about Dan?" Alex asked. "He messed up and didn't unlock the door in time. He missed his chance. So now it's impossible for him to do something good for us."

"Things are never impossible with God, Firecracker," said Father. "He can give Dan another chance. God never gives up!"

"Speaking of never giving up," said Mother, "how is your search for Nicodemus going?"

"Nicodemus!" Alex and Rudy shouted. In the excitement of being locked in the shed, they had forgotten all about the cat.

"We better go hunt some more," Alex told her brother. She jumped out of her chair. Rudy followed.

"Hold on. Hold on." Father stopped them. "Maybe Nicodemus has found his way home by now. Let's go check with Mr. Klunkett."

Alex, Rudy, and Father walked down the street to the Klunkett house. They found Mr. Klunkett watering flowers in his front yard. Alex thought he looked old and tired and sad.

"I miss that darn cat," Mr. Klunkett told them. "Nicodemus used to come outside and help me water the flowers."

"How did he help you?" Rudy looked puzzled. "A cat can't hold a hose!"

A smile crossed Mr. Klunkett's face. "No, he couldn't hold the hose. But he'd follow me around and get awfully mad if so much as a drop of water landed on him."

"Really? What did he do when he got water on him?" Rudy giggled.

"He would give me an angry look and flip his tail and stalk away," answered Mr. Klunkett.

They all laughed.

"Well, I guess that answers our question," Father told Mr. Klunkett. "We were wondering if Nicodemus had come home by himself."

"Afraid not," Mr. Klunkett sighed. "It has been real hard on Mrs. Klunkett. She just sits in front of the window, hoping to see Nicodemus. She keeps saying that he will come back to us one day."

Alex felt sorry for Mr. and Mrs. Klunkett. She hoped Mrs. Klunkett was right and Nicodemus would come home soon.

They went inside the Klunkett house. Alex and Rudy told Mr. and Mrs. Klunkett about Dan and how he had locked them in the shed that afternoon.

"Oh, dear," exclaimed Mrs. Klunkett after she had heard the story. "What a mean thing for a boy to do!"

"Dan's real mean," Alex told her. "He's the one who stole Nicodemus!"

"Now, Alex," Father cautioned. "We don't know that for sure."

"But we think he did," said Alex. "That's

why we were in Dan's yard today. We were looking for Nicodemus. Come on, Rudy, we gotta go look some more."

Alex and Rudy hurried outside. They collided with Julie and Kelli who were climbing the front steps.

"What are you doing here?" Alex asked Julie.

"Your mom said you were here," Julie answered. "Alex! Guess what? Dan hasn't come home yet and there is a police car in his driveway and policemen in his house!"

"Let's go see!" Rudy shouted and the four children raced down the street.

Alex reached Dan's house first. Two policemen were stepping outside of the house. Dan's mother followed them out of the door and onto the porch. She looked as if she had been crying.

"Don't worry, ma'am," Alex heard one of the policemen say, "we will find him."

Dan's mother watched the police car drive away. She stared down the street for a long time. She reminded Alex of a statue.

Finally, when Dan's mother turned to go back into her house, Alex caught a glimpse of her face. It was wet with tears.

"Dan is certainly causing a lot of people a lot of trouble today," Alex remarked to the others.

"I don't see why Dan's mother is so sad," Kelli commented. "I would think she would be glad to get rid of him."

"Parents are funny," Julie told her sister. "No matter what their children do, they still love them."

"Even creepy old Dan?" Kelli wrinkled her nose.

"Yes, even creepy old Dan," repeated Julie.

That night Alex lay in bed and stared at the ceiling. She could not go to sleep. She could not stop thinking about Dan and Nicodemus.

She sat up in bed and looked out of the window. It was awfully dark. She shivered to think about Dan, all by himself, wandering in the darkness. Was he afraid? Did he wish he had a friend with him?

I would be his friend if he'd let me. We

would all be his friends. But he doesn't want us to be his friends. Oh, the whole thing is impossible! Impossible! Impossible!

Alex flopped her head back onto her pillow and stared at the ceiling again. She remembered what her father had said earlier this evening—that things are never impossible with God. Maybe he was right. Maybe it all didn't look so impossible to God. Maybe God would bring Dan home. Maybe He would bring Nicodemus back to the Klunketts.

"I hope so, Heavenly Father," she whispered. "Please make everything okay."

Alex stopped worrying. She lay perfectly still. She stopped staring at the ceiling and closed her eyes. Soon, she was fast asleep.

CHAPTER 8

Wet
Journey

Alex awoke very early the next morning. She missed hearing the usual morning noises. The shower wasn't running and her mother was not clinking breakfast dishes downstairs in the kitchen.

Alex rolled over and tried to go back to sleep. But she couldn't. Finally she climbed out of bed, pulled on her clothes, and stumbled downstairs to the kitchen. She yanked a box of cereal from the cupboard and poured some with milk into a bowl. She ate quickly.

Afterwards, Alex made two peanut butter sandwiches. She packed them into her backpack along with a bottle of grape soda, a banana, potato chips, and a candy bar. She threw in a package of bubble gum. She would need lots of energy for the journey she planned to take.

Alex hoisted her pack onto her back. It was a little heavy and bulky. She wrote a note to her parents and left it on the kitchen table beside her used cereal bowl. The note read:

I have gone to look for Dan and the cat.

Love, Alex.

Alex wrote "the cat" because she wasn't sure how to spell Nicodemus. She was certain her parents would know who she meant.

Alex tiptoed to the front door and opened it softly. "No, you can't go with me," she whispered to T-Bone who had followed her to the door. "Lie down," she commanded. The puppy did as he was told but with a very sad look. Alex almost changed her mind. She would love to have her puppy along. But it wouldn't be smart to take a dog along to look for a cat!

Slipping outside, Alex hoped T-Bone would not whine or howl and wake everybody up. She felt a little guilty about leaving the house before her parents were up. She hoped they would understand. She just had to find Dan and Nicodemus.

Alex walked down the other side of the Juniper Street hill—not the side that led around the curve to Julie's and Dan's and Zack's houses, but the side that led to Kingswood Elementary School. Alex was going to check around the school for Dan.

He might go there, she thought. *There are lots of good hiding places around the school building.*

Along the way, Alex looked behind trees and bushes, searching for Nicodemus. Every so often she would stop and call, "Kitty, kitty, kitty."

Once, Alex grew excited upon hearing a "meow" sound from behind a large bush. She scurried around the bush, but was disappointed to find a black and white cat instead of an orange and white cat. The black and white cat came out from underneath the bush and rubbed her leg.

Alex gave the cat a pat. "Don't follow me," she warned it. "We don't need two cats getting lost."

Upon reaching the school, Alex ran around

to the back of the building. She cautiously climbed down the outer stairs that led to the basement door. "This would be a perfect hiding place," she told herself.

At the bottom step she stopped. The entryway was deserted. Dan was not there. Alex tried the basement door. It was locked.

With a sigh, Alex climbed back up the steps and began to circle the school building. She peeked under the loading dock. She looked into every archway and doorway. She searched the courtyard where the kindergartners played at recess. She checked the older children's playground. There was no sign of Dan.

Disappointed, Alex dropped into a swing. She had been so sure that Dan was hiding at the school. Where else could he be?

Alex gazed in all directions. Streets bordered two sides of the school. A parking lot was on the third side. Directly behind the school and beyond the playground fence, was a creek.

Alex was familiar with the creek. She loved to climb along the rocks and trees that stood along its steep banks. It would have lots of great places to hide. Maybe Dan was there!

The swing lurched as Alex leaped off it and ran to the fence. She was up and over the fence in no time. The food and bottle of grape soda rattled and gurgled in her backpack. Alex reached the creek and let her feet slide in the loose dirt all the way down its bank to the bottom.

A tiny bit of water trickled through the creek bed. An old willow tree hung over the edge of the bank, its green branches nearly touching the rocks below. Ordinarily, Alex would have swung across the creek several times on those branches. But not today. Today she was looking for Dan and Nicodemus.

Alex looked up and down the creek in both directions. Which way should she go? She remembered hearing her father say that most people turned to the right when they had to choose which way to go. "In that case," Alex decided, "I should turn to the left because Dan is not like most people." So saying, Alex turned to the left and began her journey up the creek.

She walked quickly at first, staying more or less in the middle of the creek, as the water was not deep enough to get her feet wet. She was able to scurry around several pools that blocked her path. Every so often, Alex would come across a round sewer pipe jutting out from the bank. Some of them were quite large. She carefully checked each one, making sure Dan was not hiding in one of them.

At one point, the creek bank angled sharply to the right. Concrete blocks that looked like wide steps curved into its turn. At the bottom of the "steps" was a wide pool of water. It stretched from one side of the bank to the other.

Alex stood on the edge of one of the concrete blocks and studied the pool. It was going to be hard to get around it. The pool was too wide to jump across and the banks of the creek were very steep. She decided to try climbing the right side of the bank. It had more trees and bushes to hold onto.

Grabbing a tree trunk, Alex pulled herself onto the bank. She immediately reached for the

next trunk, then a bush, and then another tree trunk. Inch by inch, Alex moved along the bank. Her feet slipped many times, and only by wrapping her arms around a tree did she save herself from sliding into the water below. Just as she thought she might make it around the pool, a branch broke and Alex tumbled down the bank and SPLASH! into the water.

"Ahhhhhh!" she screamed. The only part of her that was not covered by the cold water was her head.

Alex scrambled to her feet and leaped out of the water. She crawled to the next set of concrete blocks and lay flat on her stomach, breathing hard.

"Brussels sprouts!" she muttered. Her clothes were sopping wet and covered with mud. Water squished inside her socks and shoes. Her backpack dripped tiny drops of water onto her neck and back.

Her backpack! Alex jerked it off her back and pulled out the food she had packed. Everything seemed all right. The water had not leaked inside her pack.

Alex pulled off her tennis shoes and socks. She wrung the water out of her socks and poured it out of her shoes. She set them in the sun.

Shivering, Alex ate one partly squished peanut butter sandwich and half of the bag of potato chips. Then she drank part of the grape soda. She was tempted to eat all of the lunch she had packed.

"Why not eat it and go home?" said a voice inside her. "You are just wasting your time. You'll never find Dan or Nicodemus."

"No!" she told herself. "I will not give up. I'm gonna keep on looking."

"You could follow this creek forever and not find them," argued the voice. "You are wet and cold and miserable. Go home!"

"No!" Alex shouted. She stood up to silence the voice. "I will not quit—not yet anyway."

She gazed farther up the creek. About one hundred yards away a bridge arched over the water. Its metal sides gleamed in the sun.

"I will go as far as the bridge," Alex decided and put her wet shoes on. She gave up trying to walk on the creek bank. Instead, she splashed up the middle of the creek, the water sometimes reaching her knees.

Alex got to the bridge with no further trouble. She stood underneath it and looked up at the underside of its arch. Now what should she do? She had reached the bridge and there was still no sign of Dan or Nicodemus. Had she come all this way for nothing?

Alex sighed. Her shoulders drooped. Her legs and feet felt heavy and tired. Well, she would call Nicodemus one more time. After all, what could it hurt?

"Nicodemus!" Alex yelled. "Here, kitty, kitty, kitty!"

"Meow," squeaked a voice.

Alex whirled to her left. What she saw made her gasp out loud. There was Nicodemus, sitting tall and erect on the bank, with his tail wrapped around his feet. If it had not been for his bright yellow eyes, Alex would have almost thought she was looking at a statue. The cat's eyes stared at Alex as if to say, "What took you so long to find me?"

"Nicodemus," Alex whispered. "Kitty, kitty, kitty." She moved slowly toward the cat and reached her hand out for him.

The cat immediately flung his tail in the air and trotted a few feet up the bank.

"Nicodemus!" Alex cried. "Come back here. That's the wrong way to go!" She scrambled up the bank after the cat.

Nicodemus suddenly stopped running and rubbed his head on something. Alex stared. A shoe? Alex pulled herself further up the bank. A leg, an arm, a hand suddenly came into view. Dan? Could that be Dan?

Alex caught up with Nicodemus and gazed down at the boy lying in the brush. It was Dan! He was covered with dried mud. There was a cut on his forehead and his arms were scratched. But worst of all, his face was pale and his eyes were closed. Was he alive or was he . . . ?

CHAPTER 9

A Friend

"Brussels sprouts!" Alex gasped. She stood on the creek bank and stared at Dan. Her heart pounded with fear. He looked so . . . so still. What if he were dead? A shiver slid down Alex's back. She had never seen a dead person before.

Alex began to back away. Too late, she realized she had backed too far. With a loud cry, Alex fell over the edge of the bank and rolled down into the creek below. SPLASH! The cold water sent shivers through her entire body.

Wriggling in the sticky mud, Alex struggled out of her backpack and scrambled to her feet. She stared up at the bank and caught her breath. Dan was sitting up. He stared down at her in surprise and alarm.

"Alex?" he asked.

Alex breathed in relief. Dead boys didn't sit up and they didn't talk.

"It's me," she called to him. "I'm so glad you're alive. I mean, I thought you were dead. And I got so scared that I fell down the bank and into the creek. Brussels sprouts! This is the second time I have fallen in today!"

Dan continued to stare at her with a half-puzzled frown on his face. Then, all of a sudden, he threw back his head and laughed.

Alex laughed too—until her stomach ached. She crawled up the bank and sat down beside Dan.

"What are you doing here anyway?" Dan asked Alex.

"Looking for you," Alex replied. She began to feel nervous. She had thought only of hunting for Dan. Now that she had found him, she had no idea what to say to him.

"Why?" Dan asked.

"Why what?" Alex frowned.

"Why were you looking for me?"

"Oh," Alex tried to think of what to say.

How could she make Dan want to go back home? "Uh, I don't know," Alex began. "I just had to find you. I don't know why—maybe because God wanted me to."

"Huh? Wait a minute," Dan interrupted. "What do you mean? Why would God want you to find me?"

Alex shrugged and began kicking little rocks down the bank. "All I know is that I asked God to help me find you and He did." She looked up at Dan shyly. "God must care about you."

"God doesn't care about me!" Dan exploded. "If God cared about me, He would bring my father back to me!"

Alex was too surprised to say anything. What was Dan talking about?

"My father," Dan explained, "left me and my mom a year ago. He left us! One day he took all his stuff out of the house and disappeared. He didn't even say good-bye!" Dan's voice cracked. He sounded close to tears.

"Whew!" Alex gasped. She couldn't imagine her father leaving his family like that. Her father wouldn't do that! There was something wrong with a father who did that sort of thing.

"So," Dan continued, "if God cared about me, He would bring my father home."

"Maybe God hasn't brought your father back because he is the wrong kind of father for you," Alex said quickly.

Dan stared at her as if he had never thought of that possibility before.

"Well, it's not fair," he stormed. "Other kids have fathers. Why can't I have one?"

"You do have a Father," Alex replied, remembering her own father's words. "You have the greatest Father anyone can ever have."

"Who's that?" questioned Dan.

"God," Alex said firmly.

Dan frowned. He folded his arms across his chest and didn't say a word.

Alex was silent, too. She wondered if Dan would come home with her. She thought about his mother and her tear-streaked face. "Please, Lord Jesus, help me to get him to come home," she prayed silently.

Shifting around on the grass and leaves, Alex tried to get comfortable. She was still wet from the creek and beginning to get cold.

Suddenly, she heard a noise. She looked behind her. The bushes were moving! All at once, something orange and white shot out from a bush, leaped high in the air, and dropped gracefully to the ground on four feet.

"Nicodemus!" Alex laughed with relief. "He just caught a grasshopper!"

"He has been catching bugs all day," Dan told her. "At least he isn't going hungry."

"You mean he's eating them?" Alex cried disgustedly.

"Sure, he is," answered Dan. "He's hungry. So am I, but so far I haven't eaten any raw grasshoppers."

"Oh, gross," Alex gagged. "I think I have something better." She reached for her backpack and pulled out the rest of her lunch.

"Here, you take it," she offered. "I already had lunch."

"Really?" Dan exclaimed, staring longingly at the food.

"Sure, go ahead. You're the one who's been out all night with nothing to eat," Alex responded.

"All right!" Dan didn't wait one second longer. He gobbled down the leftover peanut butter sandwich, the potato chips, the banana, and the candy bar. He washed it down with the rest of the grape soda.

"Man, was that good!" he sighed and rubbed his stomach. "I'm sure glad you brought so much food!"

"Yeah, I thought I might find you, so I packed extra stuff," explained Alex.

"Oh, yeah?" Dan looked surprised. "Why?"

"Why what?"

"Why did you pack extra food for me? Why did you come looking for me in the first place? And why do you care anyway?" Dan narrowed his eyes and frowned at her.

Alex shrugged. "Maybe I just thought you might want a friend."

"A friend!" Dan snickered.

"Yes, a friend!" Alex repeated, angry

because Dan seemed to be making fun of her. "What's so wrong about wanting to be your friend? You could have lots of friends, you know, if you'd quit being so mean and creepy!"

Now Dan became angry. "So, what's it to you?" he shouted. "I didn't ask you to be my friend! Go away!"

"Okay! I'm going!" Alex hollered back. "You don't care about anyone! You don't even care about your own mother!"

"What do you mean my own mother?" Dan snarled. "What does my mother have to do with anything?"

"Your mother was crying! She was standing on the porch crying! I saw her!" Alex yelled. "But you don't care! Why should you care?"

Alex turned her back on Dan's shocked face. She grabbed her backpack off the ground and began running down the creek bank. In her hurry, she tripped on the strap of her pack and pitched forward. Over and over and over Alex rolled down the bank until, with a crash, she slammed into a tree trunk.

For a few moments Alex didn't move. She didn't feel as if she could move. In fact, she didn't feel anything. It was almost as though she wasn't there. Then, a sharp pain shot up her right leg.

"Ohhhhhh," she moaned and squeezed her eyes shut.

"Alex! Alex!" a voice cried above her. "Are you okay?"

Alex squinted one eye open. Dan stood over her, a worried expression on his face.

"Alex, are you okay?" he asked again. "Oh, please, be okay, Alex. I didn't mean what I said. I really do want you to be my friend."

Alex opened both eyes wide. "Really?" she asked.

"Really," Dan nodded.

At any other time, upon hearing those words, Alex would have leaped in the air with joy. But right now, her leg hurt too much.

"I don't think I can stand up," she groaned. Her right leg had been injured when she struck the tree. Now, very slowly, she stretched it out in front of her. Almost crying out from the pain, Alex bit her lip and told herself not to cry. Not in front of Dan! Not even if he was her friend.

"I don't think it's broken," Dan decided, "but I think it's going to really start swelling."

"Oh," Alex moaned.

"I know what you should do, but you aren't gonna like it," Dan warned.

"What?" Alex squeaked.

"You should put your leg in that cold water down there."

Alex made a face. "I hate that water! I've been in it twice today and it's freezing!"

"So, what's one more time?" Dan grinned. "It'll keep your leg from swelling so much."

Alex knew he was right. Her father always made her put ice on the hurts she got from playing softball.

"Oh, okay," she grumbled.

Dan held onto her right arm and tried to steady her as Alex slid, scooted, and hopped her way to the creek.

"Here, sit on this rock," Dan directed. "Put your leg all the way under the water."

Alex gritted her teeth. The cold chill crept up her entire body. After awhile, she got used to it. It really did make her leg feel better. But now, what was she going to do? She didn't think she could walk home. And what about Dan? Was he going to go home? Would he help her get home?

"Did my mom really cry?" Dan asked, interrupting Alex's thoughts.

"Huh?"

"Did my mom really stand on the porch and cry?" he asked again.

"Yeah," Alex nodded her head. "If you don't believe me, you can ask Julie and Kelli and Rudy. They saw her, too."

"Amazing," Dan whistled.

"What's so amazing about that?" Alex asked. "Mothers are supposed to feel sad if their children run away."

"Yeah, but, well, I'm always causing my mom lots of problems. You know, like I'm in trouble a lot. And, well, ever since my dad left, my mom's had to work extra hard. So I just thought that maybe she might be glad if I left.

You know, she wouldn't have to feed me or buy me clothes and stuff."

Alex wasn't sure but she thought she saw a tear slide down Dan's cheek. She stared into the water for a few moments.

"I don't think so," she finally said. "I think your mom wants you to come home."

Dan didn't answer. He busied himself by skipping small stones across the pool of water. With each skip, a little ring would form on the surface of the water. Alex watched the rings grow bigger and bigger. Soon, she was also picking up stones and side-arming them at the pool.

"How's your leg?" Dan broke the silence.

"It's okay," Alex replied. "I can't even feel it now. I guess it's too cold to feel."

"Good," replied Dan, "then we better go."

"Go where?" Alex asked.

"Home, of course," Dan answered. His face broke into a big smile.

"YAHOO!" Alex shouted. She threw handfuls of water into the air, getting both of them wet.

"Hey, cut it out," Dan laughed. "You are disturbing Nicodemus."

Alex turned around to stare at the cat. He had been sprawled on the bank sound asleep. He raised his head and stared sleepily at Alex.

"He looks real disturbed," Alex chuckled.

Dan handed Alex her backpack. She fastened it in place.

"Okay, stand up real slow on your left leg," Dan ordered.

He helped Alex to stand up, then he squatted down in front of her.

"Get on my back," he told her.

"What?" Alex exclaimed. "Piggyback?"

"Yeah, come on, I'm strong enough," Dan insisted.

Alex hopped onto his back. He got to his feet and began walking down the creek bank toward home.

"What about Nicodemus?" Alex asked worriedly.

"Call him," Dan told her. "He'll follow us."

"Kitty, kitty, kitty," Alex called.

Nicodemus slowly sat up and stretched. He
watched them walk away some distance. Then
he swooshed his tail high in the air and trotted
after them.

"I think Nicodemus likes it down here,"
Alex commented. "I don't remember him ever
being this full of energy."

Dan laughed. "Mr. Klunkett ought to take
him for walks in the creek!"

Alex grinned. She tried to picture how Mr.
Klunkett would look stomping along the creek
bank with Mrs. Klunkett buzzing behind him in

her wheelchair! Oh, the Klunketts would be so happy to get Nicodemus back. Alex nearly burst with excitement. And it was great to have Dan as a friend. Alex's grin got bigger and bigger. It was hard to believe that the same boy who had run away when Julie was caught by Mr. Klunkett was carrying her home on his back.

CHAPTER 10

Miracles

The return trip along the creek was slow. Dan could not walk very fast with Alex on his back. He had to stop many times to rest. Every time they stopped, Alex would soak her leg in the cold creek water. At last they reached the concrete blocks that marked the bend in the creek.

"Here's where I fell in the water the first time," Alex remarked. She remembered how she had been tempted to turn around and give up the search for Dan and Nicodemus. "Brussels sprouts!" she said to herself, "I'm sure glad I didn't listen to that voice."

It was about a mile from the bend in the creek back to the elementary school. By the time they reached it, Dan and Alex were exhausted. Alex was also worried. She knew she had been gone a long time. It might even be past dinnertime. Her parents must be very worried about her.

Now that they were out of the creek and onto firmer ground, Alex found she could limp beside Dan without too much pain. Dan carried Nicodemus in his arms.

Slowly, they made their way to Juniper Street. Alex gazed up its long hill and sighed.

"Do you want to stop and rest awhile?" Dan asked her.

"No, let's get it over with," Alex gritted her teeth and began the climb.

"HEY!" a voice suddenly cried out. "ALEX, IS THAT YOU?"

"IT'S ALEX!" someone else shouted.

Running feet pounded down the hill toward Alex and Dan. It was Zack, Mark, Julie, and Kelli. Behind them ran Rudy and (Alex gasped) her father!

Alex felt Dan stiffen beside her. She was almost afraid that he might suddenly run in the other direction. But he didn't. He stood beside Alex and waited for the others to reach them.

The other children stopped a few feet away from Alex and Dan. No one spoke. They waited for Alex's father to catch up.

Father walked up to Alex and Dan. He looked stern but Alex could see the twinkle in his eye and knew that somewhere behind that stern look lay a hidden smile.

Father held out his hand to Dan. "Thank you for bringing Alex home, Dan," he said.

Dan timidly shook Father's hand. "Uh," he stammered, "I think it was the other way around. She brought me home."

Father laughed. He swooped Alex into his arms and hugged her tightly. "I'm so proud of you, Firecracker," he whispered in her ear.

"You mean you're not mad at me for being so late getting home?" Alex asked.

"Mad?" Father repeated. "No, I wasn't mad. But to tell you the truth, I was rather worried. And so was your mother. Come on, we better go show her that you are okay."

"I'm okay, except for my leg," Alex told him. "I twisted it and Dan had to carry me on his back all the way down the creek."

Father raised his eyebrows at Dan. "That took some muscle, I'd say." He put his arm across Dan's shoulders and they started up the hill together.

Alex, still in her father's arms, squeezed his neck tightly. Didn't he always know the right thing to do? He hadn't yelled or got mad or anything. Instead, he had shaken Dan's hand and now he was walking with him up the hill!

When they reached the top of the hill, Mother ran to meet them. "Oh, Alex, I'm so glad you are safe!" she cried. "I was so worried about you." She grabbed Alex out of Father's arms and held her close.

"I'm okay, Mom, except for a hurt leg," Alex managed to mumble in between her mother's kisses.

"We better take a look at that leg," Father chuckled. "Come on inside, Dan. We can call your mother from our house."

Dan didn't move. He held the cat tightly and stared down the street at the Klunketts' house.

"There's something I need to do first," he replied softly.

Alex knew what that was. "I'll go with you," she offered.

"No thanks," Dan answered. "I think I should do it alone."

"I'll wait right here for you," she told him. "I won't leave and if you need any help, just call me."

Dan smiled. "You're a good friend, Alex," he said.

Alex sat down on the sidewalk. Father and Mother sat down beside Alex. Rudy and the other children joined them. Nobody said a word. They watched as Dan made his way to the Klunketts' front door.

Mr. Klunkett opened the door. Alex felt a shiver of excitement. She heard Mr. Klunkett exclaim, "Nicodemus!" Then Dan and Nicodemus disappeared into the Klunketts' house. The door closed. The street was empty and silent.

"Brussels sprouts! I can't stand it!" Alex hollered and tilted backwards in a sprawl on the sidewalk.

Father chuckled. "It seems to me that this is

the second time one of your friends has disappeared through Mr. Klunkett's front door."

"Right," Alex groaned, "and I'm always left outside to worry about them."

But she didn't have to worry for very long. After a few minutes, Mr. Klunkett opened his front door and stepped outside. He waved his arms and called to them.

"I guess that's our signal," grinned Father.

"Let's go," Alex cried. She raced as fast as she could go to the Klunketts' house, ignoring her hurt leg. The others hurried along behind her.

When Alex burst through the door, she found Dan sitting on a stool by the window. Next to him sat Mrs. Klunkett in her wheelchair. In Mrs. Klunkett's lap, snuggled a big orange and white cat.

Tears of happiness slid down Mrs. Klunkett's face. She smiled at Alex and reached for her hand. Seeing the joy in Mrs. Klunkett's eyes made all the worry, the tiredness, and the ache in Alex's leg disappear. It had all been worth it.

"Alex," Mrs. Klunkett said, "Dan has told me how you searched for him and Nicodemus, and how you found them and brought them home. I thank you from the bottom of my heart."

Alex grinned and hugged Mrs. Klunkett. Mrs. Klunkett hugged Dan. Then, Mr. Klunkett hugged all three of them. There were many smiles and many happy tears.

Dan called his mother who rushed to the Klunkett house immediately. She threw her arms around her son and cried tears of joy. Alex was sure that Dan could have no doubts about his mother wanting him home.

As everyone sat in the Klunketts' living room, Father joked, "Well, this has certainly become the neighborhood meeting place."

"Yeah," Rudy piped up. "When are you going to pass out your mint cookies?" he asked Mrs. Klunkett.

"Rudy!" Mother exclaimed, embarrassed.

Mrs. Klunkett laughed. "I just happen to have made a double batch today. Rudy, would you like to help me bring them in?"

Rudy helped Mrs. Klunkett pass around plates filled with mint cookies. Everyone helped themselves. However, no one ate as many as Dan and Alex.

"I do believe these cookies are becoming quite famous," Father winked at Rudy.

Suddenly, Nicodemus sprang out of Mrs. Klunkett's lap and bounded toward the bookcase.

"Look!" Rudy cried. "He's going up his stairway."

Sure enough, the big cat climbed quickly up

the miniature stairway to the top shelf. He plopped himself down on the shelf and stretched out a paw to bat one of his toys.

"Oh dear!" Mrs. Klunkett cried. "I must hurry." She zoomed her wheelchair over to the bookcase just in time to catch the little red ball as it sailed off the shelf and into her lap.

Everyone laughed at Nicodemus' trick. Alex thought Nicodemus looked very pleased with himself.

Later, as everyone was saying their good-byes, Alex heard Mr. Klunkett ask, "Will you come and see me tomorrow morning, Dan?" She saw Dan nod his head.

On the way home she asked her father, "Do you think Mr. Klunkett might become Dan's father figure?"

Father looked surprised. "Why do you say that, Firecracker?" he asked.

"Because Mr. Klunkett wants Dan to come and see him tomorrow," she replied.

"Hmmm," Father stroked his chin. "Maybe so."

The next morning Alex answered the front

doorbell to find Dan standing on her front porch. He was holding a tiny orange and white kitten in his arms.

"Hi, Alex! How do you like my new kitten?" grinned Dan.

"Your kitten?" she exclaimed. "Is that your kitten?"

"Yeah, Mr. Klunkett gave him to me this morning," Dan said proudly.

"Fantastic!' Alex cried. "He looks just like Nicodemus. Where did Mr. Klunkett get him?"

"From the Animal Shelter. Mr. Klunkett said he went there this morning to find a kitten. They had a whole cage of them. He said he picked out the one that looked the most like Nicodemus."

"What are you going to name him?" Alex asked Dan.

"Nicky, of course, after Nicodemus," replied Dan.

"I'm sure Nicodemus will be very honored," Alex giggled.

"Well, I gotta go now," Dan told her. "Mr. Klunkett wants me to help him put together a new train engine."

"You know, Mom," Alex said to her mother after Dan had left, "this may sound strange, but Dan seems like a different person. Even his face looks different—kind of sunshiny and real happy."

"I think I know what you mean," her mother replied. "Lots of times our feelings show on our faces—like sadness or happiness. Right now Dan's face shows how happy he is to find out that people love and care for him."

"Yeah," Alex smiled, "I guess God made us that way so that when we see somebody with a sad face, we can help them."

"I think you are right, honey," Mother gave Alex a hug. "I am sure that God is very happy with the way you have helped Dan."

Alex smiled. "God has done lots of miracles in Dan's life. And He answered all of my prayers! God helped me to find Dan. He made Dan my friend and made him want to come home with me. He gave him Mr. Klunkett as a father figure. And, He even gave Dan a kitten!"

Mother laughed again.

"Mom?" Alex began, "Can we get a—"

"No, Alex," her mother answered before Alex could finish.

"How did you know what I was going to say?" Alex demanded.

"You were going to ask me if we could get one of those orange and white kittens," her mother smiled.

"Well, can we?" Alex asked hopefully.

"No, Alex, not right now," Mother replied. "Not until T-Bone is more grown up. He would accidentally stomp on a kitten and hurt it."

Alex frowned down at her puppy. He lay at her feet with his chin flat on the floor between his front paws. He rolled his eyes up at her with a very sad expression.

"He looks like he knows what you just said," Alex told her mother.

Alex and Mother giggled.

Just then the front door flew open and Alex's older sister, Barbara, stumbled inside. She banged her suitcases down on the floor in front of Alex and Mother. "I just hated to leave the Ozarks," she sighed. "It was so exciting. I don't suppose anything exciting has happened around here while I was gone."

Alex and Mother looked at each other and burst out laughing. "Just wait until we tell you all that has happened!" they exclaimed.

Amen.